CAUTION: SMALL ENSEMBLES

CARTOONS BY EDWARD KOREN
PANTHEON BOOKS NEW YORK

To Curtis and Nat and Sasha

By the same author
Are You Happy?
Well, There's Your Problem

Compilation copyright © 1983 by Edward Koren

All rights reserved under International and Pan-American Copyright
Conventions. Published in the United States by Pantheon Books,
a division of Random House, Inc., New York, and simultaneously
in Canada by Random House of Canada Limited, Toronto.

All of the drawings in this collection appeared originally
in The New Yorker and were copyrighted © 1980, 1981,
1982, and 1983 by The New Yorker Magazine, Inc.

Library of Congress Cataloging in Publication Data
Koren, Edward.
Caution: small ensembles.
1. American wit and humor, Pictorial.   I. Title.
NC1429.K62A4   1983   741.5'973   83-8225
ISBN 0-394-53322-4

Manufactured in the United States of America

First Edition

"I'm in here—luxuriating."

"I'm sorry—I feel uncomfortable talking about sex."

"And please don't hesitate to call on us. Our dedicated staff will be delighted to serve you."

"He's a very fussy eater."

"I'm sure you don't recognize my son."

"How old is your cabbage?"

"I've been a great admirer of your work for years.
It's a real pleasure to meet you."
"I'm happy to meet _you_. I'm your biggest fan."

"Could we have a little eye contact?"

"Mr. Thomas and Mr. Robbins occupy themselves with my personal safety."

"We had a hunch they'd be perfect for each other."

"You'll find there's no right or wrong here. Just what works for _you_."

"*For me, this section of Bloomingdale's is* terra incognita."

"The service is polite and well meaning, if a little slow."

"That's a bird, spelled b-i-r-d."

"I'm a party of one."

"The institution of marriage gets a big boost from you folks."

"Your invitation said bring a spouse or friend. This is my friend."

"Professor Farrow, this afternoon's guest speaker, is steady and reliable and unswayed by trendy thinking."

"This is one of the theater's great exit scenes."

"David, you're denying your feelings again, aren't you?"

*"My darling, I want to share my money worries, my tensions,
and my unhappiness with you for the rest of my life."*

"Mother of four, meet mother of three."

"We're just family."

"You will find that our colleague to my left is no receiver of idées reçues."

"You two should have met a long time ago—Light n' Lively, this is Crisp n' Crunchy."

"I'm sorry, I don't like men with moustaches."

"We never laugh together anymore."

"I'm indoorsy and Paul is outdoorsy."

"I want to be able to speak the desperate things the heart feels."

"All right, food people—are you ready?"

"James, James, it's only foreign policy."

"I spent most of my time this summer gardening and cooking,
and Charles answered his mail."

"Bob, we've asked you to join us today because you have no personality, no ideas, and you're a bit of a wimp."

"Can I call you back? Jim and I are struggling with our roles."

"And now for the taste test."

"How long do you like the cuffs?"

"You have to understand that pain, anger, and suffering are part of the human condition."

"Your instructions were perfect."

"We are looking for the non-yucky apparel."

"Richard is a nostalgia person."

FELTSVILLE
GENERAL STORE
YOU ARE
NOT
WELCOME
TO
FELTSVILLE
TURN AROUND!
GO AWAY!
VAMOOSE!
GET OUT!
THE XENOPHOBIA CAPITAL
OF THE U.S.A.

"You've been a very, _very_ bad sibling."

"I'd like to tell you about our specials this evening."

"At great personal risk, I'd like to compliment you on your perfume."

"You know, this is my oldest friend."

"Watch out. The cognoscenti are not pleased."

"Does anyone mind if I smoke?"

"This is my slender volume of poems."

"I'm very, very fussy when it comes to men."

"Hugh understands wood."

"Everything's just fine. The garden is coming in beautifully, and Jeremy is in his usual rage."

"This is our collection of miniatures."

"I want national recognition for the problems I've had with him."

"What a pleasure to find someone else who detests digital watches."

"This is my new friend—Michael. We cook together."

"Nan, your cassoulet is superb—from a feminist perspective, of course."

"You've got an irate client on 3, an impatient supplier on 1, an anxious child on 5, and an angry wife on 2."

"The sunsets here are amazing."

"Is <u>this</u> the underrated Donald Rice?"

"Here to share their thoughts and feelings with us this evening are
Jackie Parsons-Wilder, Eugenia Robbins-Randolph, Sarah Brundelmeyer-
Hurd, Rachel Rice-Grant, and Jane Thomaston-Whitehouse-Morgenthaller."

"Isn't it astonishing that no two of us are exactly alike?"

"Nicholas, you are to address me as 'Larry,' not 'sir.' Is that clear?"

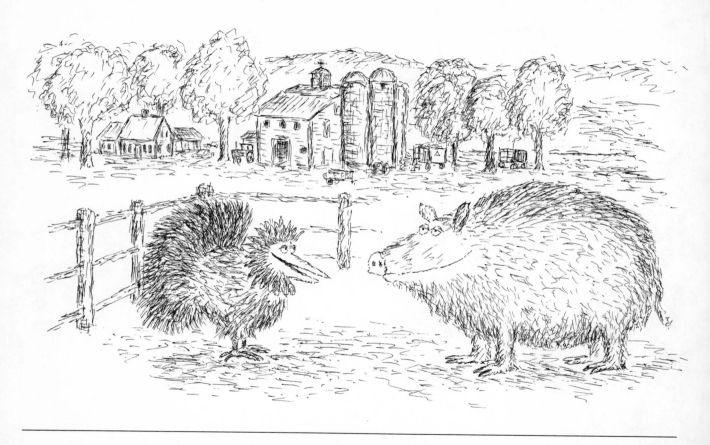

"My friend, you are weighty in form but light in content."

"You two are perfect for a folie à deux."

"Could we have a soupçon of Debussy?"

"I'd like to humanize you."

"Leslie and I were married last week, but she's refusing to take my name."

"*That's* fathering."

"Do you know how masculine it is to risk crying?"

"Ooh! How <u>cute</u>!"

"My dog's name is Kierkegaard, my cat is named Virginia Woolf,
I call my car Amadeus, and my boyfriend's name is Freddy."

"I've spent this past year working on myself."

"Stephen is self-absorbed, Judith is self-conscious, Dick is self-critical, and Catherine is self-assured."

"Don't worry. He doesn't bite."

"You've got to admit we look good together."

"Why don't you leave your worries behind you and have something from the bar?"

"People who wish to register their irritation should go to Room 203.
People who want to express their anger should proceed to Room 210.
And those who would like to give vent to their frustration must wait here."

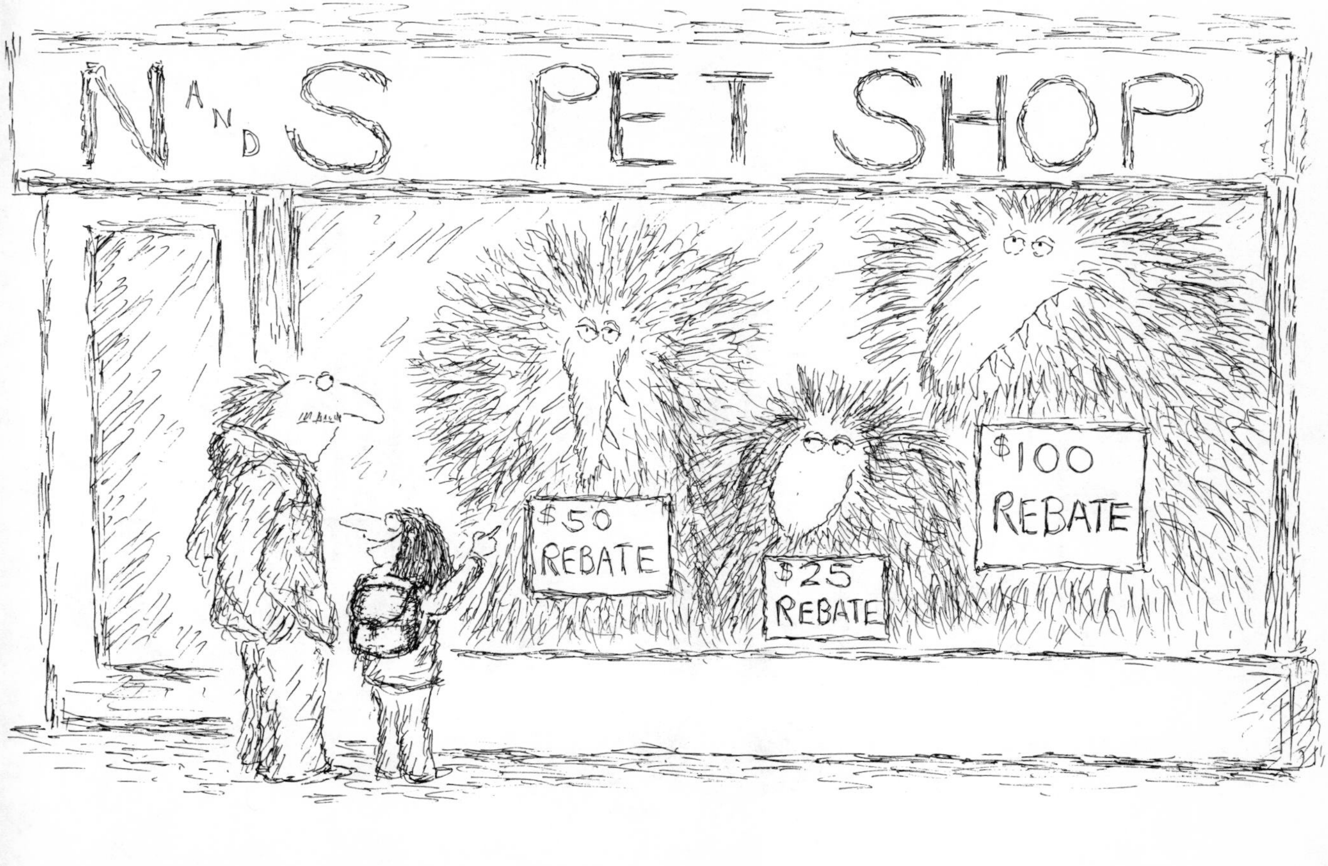
N AND S PET SHOP
$50 REBATE
$25 REBATE
$100 REBATE